CHOO CHOO
Clickety-clack!

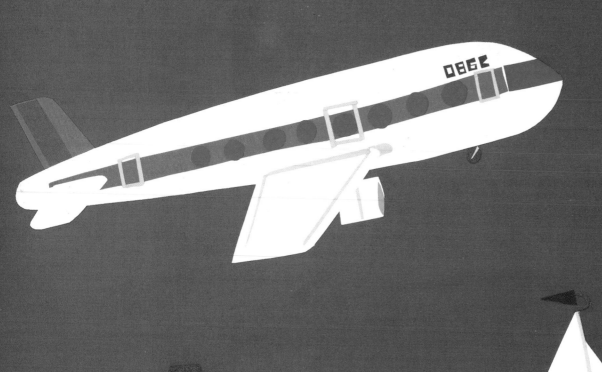

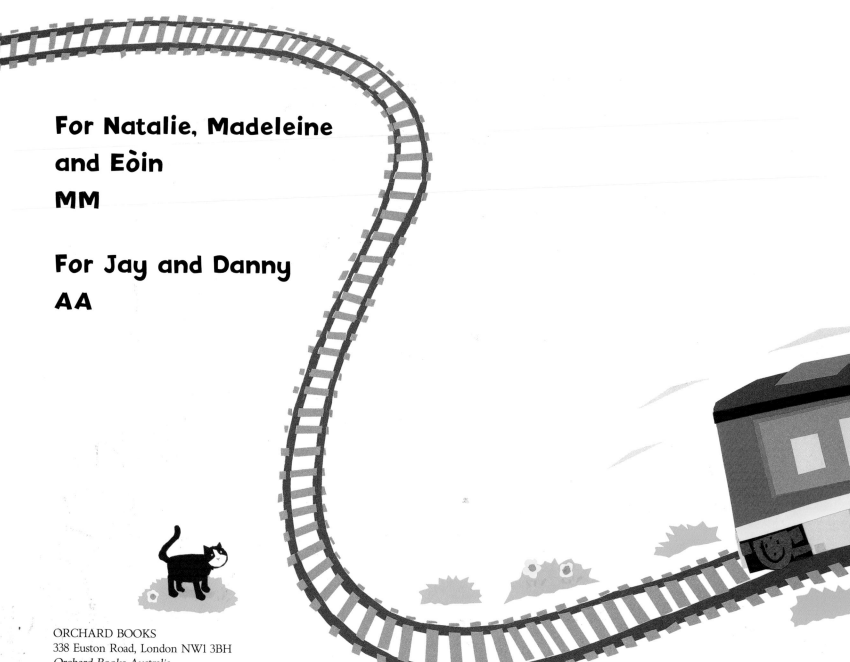

For Natalie, Madeleine and Eòin
MM

For Jay and Danny
AA

ORCHARD BOOKS
338 Euston Road, London NW1 3BH
Orchard Books Australia
Level 17/207 Kent Street, Sydney, NSW 2000
First published by Orchard Books in 2004
First published in paperback in 2005
ISBN 978 1 84362 438 7
Text © Margaret Mayo 2004
Illustrations © Alex Ayliffe 2004
The rights of Margaret Mayo to be identified as the author
and of Alex Ayliffe to be identified as the illustrator
of this work have been asserted by them in accordance
with the Copyrights, Designs and Patents Act, 1988.
A CIP catalogue record of this book is available from the British Library.
20 19 18 17 16 15 14 13 12
Printed in China
Orchard Books is a division of Hachette Children's Books,
an Hachette UK company.
www.hachette.co.uk

CHOO CHOO
clickety-clack!

written by **Margaret Mayo**   illustrated by **Alex Ayliffe**

ORCHARD

Trains are great at speed, speed, **speeding,**
Tooting - wh**ooo**-h**ooo**!
Through tunnels rattling, at stations stopping;
Choo choo, clickety-clack! Off they go!

Aeroplanes are great at fly, fly, flying,
To faraway places people carrying,
Zooming down runways – up, up and away – soaring;
WhoarrrRR! Off they go!

Cars are great at drive, drive, **driving,**
To shops, to friends or a special outing,
Quick packing, seats choosing, belts fastening;
Beep-beep! Off they go!

Racing cars are great at race, race, **racing**, waiting at the starting line, crouching, growling, Hurtling round the track, chase, chase, chasing; **Grrumm, grrumm! Off they go!**

Sailing boats are great at sail, sail, sailing,
Over waves bouncing,
Water slap-slapping, sails flapping;
Flappety-flap! Off they go!

Hot-air balloons are great at float, float, floating,

High in the sky glide, gliding.

Filling, swelling and rising;

Whoo-oosh! Off they go!

Motorbikes are great at roar, roar, **roaring,**

swooping, swerving and overtaking.

Careful now – no crashing!

Vroom, vroom! Off they go!

Cycles are great at whiz, whiz, **whizzing,**

They have no engines, just pedals for pushing,

But they shoot by, wheels whirl, whirling;
Zippety-zip! Off they go!

Cable cars are great at climb, climb, climbing,
Up the mountain swiftly swinging.
Hurry in, skiers – doors closing;
Shlummp! Whurr-rr! Off they go!

Buses are great at travel, travel, **travelling**,
Always at the same time, the same route following,
Ding-ding! Always stopping and starting;
Brumm, brumm! **Off they go!**

Ferryboats are great at load, load, **loading,**
Cars and trucks parking, people boarding.

Ready to leave! Pomp, **pomp,** hooter sounding;
Chug, chug! Off they go!

Now it is dark – many vehicles are resting,
But some keep travelling just as fast,
Still zoom-zooming and clickety-clacking;
On they go till they are **home at last!**